Westland City Ordinance 62-132
Protects the Library from the theft of library materials and/or conversion of those materials to personal use.

Failure to Return Items When Due shall make you guilty of a misdemeanor.
Please Return Your Materials!

The Gecko

A Dillon Remarkable Animals Book

The Gecko

By Victoria Sherrow

DILLON PRESS, INC.
Minneapolis, Minnesota 55415

Photographic Acknowledgments

The photographs are reproduced through the courtesy of: Fred Dodd/International Zoological Expeditions; Gerry Ellis/Ellis Wildlife Collection; Breck P. Kent; Robert and Linda Mitchell; Brian Parker/Tom Stack and Associates. Cover photograph by Breck P. Kent.

Library of Congress Cataloging-in-Publication Data

Sherrow, Victoria.
   The gecko / by Victoria Sherrow.
      p.   cm. — (A Dillon remarkable animals book)
   Includes bibliographical references.
   Summary: Examines the physical characteristics, habits, and natural environments of several members of the 600-plus species of the small lizard that inhabits every continent on earth except Antarctica.
ISBN 0-87518-4413 (lib. bdg.) : $12.95
   1. Geckos—Juvenile literature. [1. Geckos. 2. Lizards.]
   I. Title. II. Series.
QL666.L245S34   1990
597.95—dc 20   90-3283
                                                                        CIP
                                                                         AC

© 1990 by Dillon Press, Inc. All rights reserved

Dillon Press, Inc., 242 Portland Avenue South
Minneapolis, Minnesota 55415

Printed in the United States of America
1 2 3 4 5 6 7 8 9 10 99 98 97 96 95 94 93 92 91 90

Contents

Facts about the Gecko 6
1. A Noisy Acrobat 9
2. A Special Reptile 21
3. Life in the Tropics 33
4. From Egg to Adult 41
5. People and Geckos 49
Glossary 55
Index 58

Facts about Geckos

Scientific Name: *Gekkonidae*

Description:

Length—Adults vary in length from about 2 to 14 inches (5 to 35 centimeters), depending on the species; adults of most species are between 3 to 6 inches (7.5 to 15 centimeters)

Weight—From 1 ounce to about 9 ounces (28 to 252 grams)

Physical Features—Toes are usually equipped with toe pads as well as claws; large eyes with big pupils; soft skin with small scales

Color—Varies widely depending upon the species; green, brown, yellow, and many other colors

Distinctive Habits: Able to "speak" by clicking its tongue; species with clinging toe pads can run up vertical surfaces and upside down on ceilings

Food: Insects; a few species eat fruit and flower nectar

Reproductive Cycle: In cooler climates, males and females mate in the spring; mate throughout the year in tropical climates; two eggs are laid on land and left alone to hatch

Life Span: Varies with the species; usually about seven to nine years

Range: Tropical and warm temperate regions; most numerous near the equator—southwestern deserts of the United States (western Texas, New Mexico, southern Arizona); southern California; Florida and Florida Keys; Cuba; Central America; South America; Caribbean and Pacific islands; Galapagos Islands; New Zealand; Australia; Sumatra, Iran; Africa; India; southern Asia; East Indies; one species in the Himalayan mountains

The shaded areas on this map show the range of the gecko.

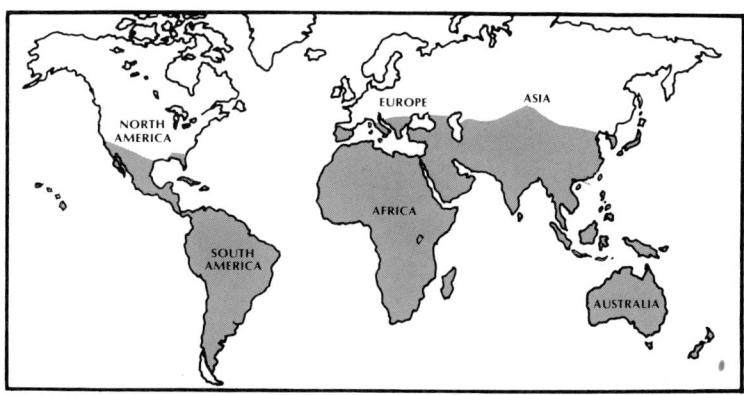

The Trinidad day gecko opens its mouth to chatter.

Chapter 1

A Noisy Acrobat

It is nighttime in a tropical **rain forest**.* The air is warm and moist as the sun sinks behind the thick umbrella of leaves. From a branch of a palm tree comes a strange cry, *Yech-oh! Yech-oh!*

What animal is making such a racket? It is not a bird or a frog. This noisy creature is a small lizard called a gecko.

Different types of geckos make different sounds. Some bark, chirp, or croak. Others squeak or screech. Various geckos make a sound like, *Geck-oh!* That is how this family of lizards got its unusual name.

Chattering geckos are heard around the world, and not only in tropical forests. They live on every continent except Antarctica. Geckos are seen in

*Words in **bold type** are explained in the glossary at the end of this book.

The Gecko

Africa and Asia, the southwestern United States, and on islands in the Atlantic and Pacific oceans.

The gecko is the noisiest of all lizards. It is also one of nature's most amazing climbers. This nimble creature crawls up tree trunks and the walls of buildings. It can climb up a pane of glass and walk upside down across a ceiling!

Why All The Noise?

Tkk-tkkk! Tsee-tsee! Chee-yak! These are some noises that different geckos make. The gecko "speaks" by clicking its thick tongue against the roof of its mouth.

Scientists are not sure what all of the sounds mean. Some geckos make noise when they hunt and capture insects. Many cry out in times of danger, squeaking if they are grabbed by humans or **predators**.

Geckos are quite noisy, too, when they defend their **territory**, especially a feeding place. They often try to scare away other animals by acting

This day gecko screeches loudly to protect its territory.

fierce. They open their eyes and mouths wide, then thrust their bodies forward and make barking sounds. The other animal is often so startled that it backs away.

Geckos also call out during the mating season. Male African and Asian house geckos make shrill sounds. Other **species**, or kinds, of the lizard,

The Gecko

such as the Indian wall gecko, click their tongues during courtship. Both males and females make these noises with their tongues.

Fancy Feet

Most geckos have feet that are designed for climbing on smooth surfaces. Geckos have four feet, with five wide, flat toes on each foot. On the bottom of each toe is a pad, covered with thousands of hooklike hairs. The hairs are so small that they can be seen only with a **microscope**.

These hairy toe pads cling to tiny cracks and other slightly uneven areas on windows, walls, or ceilings. A layer of dust on a dry window is enough for a toe pad to cling to.

The gecko has a body designed to move quickly and in unusual ways. Some people think that the gecko wiggles in a funny way as it scurries up a wall or across a ceiling. This is probably because it must unhook its clinging toe pads after every step. With a rapid motion, the gecko lifts up

A Tokay gecko, with its hairy toe pads, easily climbs up a pane of glass.

its toes, then presses them down again, step after step. Its nimble feet allow the gecko to chase insects swiftly and to outrun many enemies.

Some geckos are **arboreal**, meaning they live in trees. These geckos use their claws to climb. All geckos have claws—one at the end of each toe. They snap out, like those of a cat, when the lizard

An underside view of a gecko's clinging toe pads.

needs to grip rough surfaces such as tree bark.

With its toe pads and claws, the gecko moves easily and quickly from one surface to another. It is astonishing to watch these small creatures scurry up a wall, across a ceiling, and then down the wall on the other side of the room!

A Noisy Acrobat

A Talented Tail

Arboreal geckos use their tails to help them balance in trees. The tail is like an extra leg. It wraps around branches or leaves, helping the gecko to hang on. A tail that is used in this way is called a **prehensile** tail.

Geckos also use their tails to protect themselves. Although geckos see well and move swiftly, they are often caught and eaten by larger animals such as birds and rats. But if an animal seizes a gecko's tail, the lizard easily escapes. It simply twists its body so the brittle bones in its tail break, and the tail falls off.

The broken tail keeps wiggling for several minutes, as if it were alive. While the rat or bird eats the tail, the gecko runs away. Later, a new tail grows on the gecko. It will not look perfect, but it will be close to the same shape as the old one.

Keen Night Vision

Most geckos are **nocturnal**, meaning they are

The Gecko

active at night. Their eyes are designed for seeing well in the dark. At night, the gecko's large pupils open wide to let in as much light as possible.

Certain sense cells in the gecko's eye pick up faint light very well. All eyes contain sense cells called **rods** and **cones**. Rods and cones are connected to nerves that carry messages to the brain. In the dark, rods carry messages better than cones. Like the eyes of other nocturnal animals, the gecko's eyes contain a rich supply of rods.

Some species of geckos are active in the daytime instead of at night. They must be able to protect their eyes from bright sunshine. In bright light, the gecko's pupils close up and become thin, vertical slits. The pupils close almost completely. This is important, because the gecko does not have ordinary eyelids that shut when the sun is too bright. A gecko's eyelids are transparent, like glass. They do not open and close like a human's eyelids, but are fixed in place.

The gecko's see-through eyelids are called **spec-**

The gecko's pupil closes up in bright sunlight.

tacles. How does the lizard keep its spectacles clean? It uses its tongue to wipe away dust and other dirt. Flick, flick, flick! The tongue works like a built-in windshield wiper.

The gecko's keen daytime and nighttime vision helps it to catch insects for food and to avoid its enemies. The little lizard's hairy toe pads and

A Noisy Acrobat

removable tails also help it to survive in the wild.
    Yeck-oh! Yeck-oh! To-kay! To-kay! Chee-yak! Chu-chu! The calls of these small, noisy lizards are heard mainly after dark, and in warm regions throughout the world.

A Tokay gecko washes its eye with its tongue.

Chapter 2

A Special Reptile

Millions of years ago, dinosaurs roamed the earth. It may be hard to believe that the tiny geckos could be related to the huge dinosaurs. But they are. Dinosaurs and geckos belong to the same class of animals, known as reptiles. This name comes from the Latin word *repere*, meaning "to creep."

Reptiles are divided into four different groups, or **orders**. One of these orders is called *squamata*. Geckos, all other lizards, and snakes belong to squamata—the largest of the four groups of reptiles. About 90 percent of all reptiles belong to this order.

Reptiles are cold-blooded animals. Like all reptiles, the cold-blooded gecko does not produce its own body heat the way a warm-blooded animal does. It cannot keep its body warmer or cooler than

The Texas Banded gecko is a small relative of the dinosaurs.

The Gecko

the air around it. The gecko must live in a warm climate, such as in the tropics. Here, air temperatures are warm year-round, even at night.

The gecko uses the sun's energy to heat its body. The lizard sunbathes on warm rocks, sand, or tree branches to soak up warmth. Then, if it gets too hot, it moves to a cooler spot. Geckos that live in tropical forests cool off under leaves or rocks.

Some geckos also live on the sand dunes, rocky areas, and canyon beds of deserts. They must work hard to keep an even body temperature in this hot, dry climate. They burrow under sand to keep cool. These geckos are found in the deserts of Mexico and North and South Africa. They also live in the deserts of the southwestern United States—in Arizona, California, Texas, Utah, Nevada, and New Mexico.

New Skin and Scales

Most reptiles, including geckos, have dry, shell-like skin covered with scales. The thick outer layer of

It is now the time of year for the Mediterranean gecko to shed and grow new skin.

skin is made of dead cells and **keratin**, a tough substance found in fingernails, feathers, and horns. This outer layer holds moisture inside the gecko's body so the lizard does not become too dry.

Small scales cover the gecko's soft skin. Several times a year, the gecko sheds its old skin. A desert gecko may shed even more often.

The Gecko

Shedding helps geckos to stay clean. Casting off their old skin gets rid of **parasites**. Parasites are tiny creatures, such as mites, that live on larger animals. Mites and other types of parasites suck the blood of the bigger animal.

The gecko begins to shed after new scales grow under its old skin. Unlike snakes that lose their skin in one piece, the gecko sheds in patches. The lizard scratches itself to help the top layer fall off. Geckos often eat pieces of their old skin, too. Some **herpetologists**, people who study reptiles, think the lizards eat the old layer because it contains useful **nutrients**.

Some Members of the Family

There are hundreds of species of this little reptile. The various species have special traits—such as flat feet for running on sand—that help them survive in different regions. About 750 species of geckos can be found around the world. Many look very different from each other.

The Reef gecko is the smallest species of gecko.

The Reef gecko is the smallest of all the species. An adult measures less than two inches (five centimeters) in length. It lives in Cuba, Florida, and the Bahama Islands. The Reef gecko is not only the smallest gecko, it is the smallest reptile in the world.

Some of the most colorful geckos are the day geckos. They live on Madagascar and Mauritius,

The Gecko

near Africa in the Indian Ocean. Day geckos are usually about 4.5 inches (11 centimeters) long. Some are bright green with blue-green backs and red stripes that decorate their heads, bodies, and tails. Day geckos eat fruit as well as insects.

The Tokay gecko that lives in Asia is the largest of all the species. It was named for its call, *To-kay! To-kay!* The average adult Tokay is about 12 to 14 inches (30 to 35 centimeters) long. It has yellow eyes, and gray-blue skin with rust or reddish spots. The Tokay lives in Asia. It eats small mice, insects, and other types of lizards. For this reason, people often allow it to live in their homes.

Another unusual species lives in Africa. It is called the Leopard gecko. Its coloring is similar to a spotted leopard. This gecko's skin is brown or yellow and covered with black spots.

Other geckos are known for their strange-looking tails. The Apple-leaf tail gecko has a wide, flat tail that looks like the leaf of an apple tree. The tail of the Scallop-tailed gecko has curved edges like a

A colorful day gecko in Madagascar.

shell. Two species with bumpy tails are called Turnip-tail geckos and Knob-tailed geckos.

Two other species of geckos are known for the expressions on their faces. The Velvet gecko of Africa always appears to be smiling! The Sad gecko of Asia has a mouth that tilts down, giving the lizard an unhappy look.

The Gecko

The Flying gecko of Java has unusual folds of skin on the sides of its body, tail, and legs. Small folds on the feet make them look webbed. These skin flaps work like parachutes as this lizard leaps from one tree branch to another.

Several desert species live in the southwestern United States. Desert geckos have slender toes without toe pads. Their flatter feet help them to run across fine desert sand. Their skin is brown and tan, matching the sandy, rocky regions where they live.

The Banded gecko lives in desert areas of Utah, California, and Arizona. It is about 5 inches (12.5 centimeters) long. This gecko moves its tail back and forth when it chases insects for food. It makes a chirping noise when it is caught by an enemy.

The Big-bend geckos of Texas and Mexico are about 6 inches (15 centimeters) long. Unlike many other species, the eyelids of the Big-bend gecko are able to open and close.

A Special Reptile

It lives in Louisiana, too. This species came to the United States from southern Europe, which is how it got its name. Mediterranean geckos live on palm trees and in houses. They are about 4.5 inches long and have white or pink skin. They are very active at night, chasing insects around lighted areas. The males of this species squeak loudly when other geckos hunt for food in their territory.

In spite of their very different colors and features, these lizards are all geckos. They are small relatives of the dinosaurs and special members of the class of animals called reptiles.

Chapter 3

Life in the Tropics

The geckos' calls are heard in warm regions around the world—in forests, jungles, mountains, swamps, islands, and deserts. How did geckos come to live in so many places on earth, including islands out in the ocean?

Through the centuries, geckos have traveled on ships, logs, and plants that floated out to sea. Others traveled to new places on cargo ships loaded with produce or timber.

Gecko eggs travel, too. The shells are often sticky and easily become attached to logs and plants that float to islands or other lands. The baby geckos that hatch in these new places sometimes survive if the climate and conditions are right.

In the past, species of geckos, such as this day gecko of Madagascar, traveled to islands out in the ocean.

Finding Food

Geckos that live in the tropics enjoy a large supply of insects. Tropical trees keep their leaves all year, and attract many bugs. The insects feed on the trees' growing leaves.

The gecko, in turn, feeds on the bugs. Flies, locusts, crickets, mosquitoes, moths, cockroaches, and maggots are among the geckos' **prey** in these warm regions.

Many people who live in tropical areas are glad to have geckos nearby, even living inside their homes. They get rid of troublesome insects in houses and gardens.

Tropical geckos often live in houses and other buildings. They hide in thatched roofs or in the cracks of walls.

At night, lights in the buildings attract insects. The gecko chases the bugs across walls and ceilings, seizing them for a meal. A gecko may like a particular home with its tasty supply of insects so much that it stays there, like a pet.

A day gecko enjoys a grasshopper meal.

Watch Out for Predators!

Geckos do enjoy a rich supply of insects and a warm, moist climate in the tropics. In these ways, life in such areas is easy. But in other ways, life is difficult here. Tropical forests contain more kinds of animals than any other place on earth. Some of these animals are predators of the gecko. They hunt and kill the lizard for food.

The Gecko

The gecko's predators include frogs, snakes, rats, birds, and larger lizards. During the hours when they are not active, geckos hide from their enemies. They seek cover in cracks in buildings, under rocks and leaves, and in holes in the sand. Their soft, flat bodies allow them to squeeze into narrow spaces.

Some geckos rely on **camouflage** to avoid being caught. The colors and markings on their skin blend with their natural surroundings. The Central American Forest gecko is a good example. It hides from its enemies by resting quietly on the forest floor, its black and tan skin blending with the shadows, wood chips, and plant growth. Predators pass by without noticing it.

Another well-camouflaged species is the bright green Madagascar day gecko. Its color makes it hard to see on the leafy trees where it lives.

The skin of many geckos, such as the green-eyed Giant gecko of Asia, looks like tree bark. Their brown or gray skin with its barklike mark-

The skin of the Central American Forest gecko blends with the wood chips on the forest floor.

ings helps keep them hidden on branches and tree trunks. These geckos press their bodies and tails closely against the side of a tree. Their skin and the bark blend together, and they appear invisible to their predators. Often camouflage helps these lizards catch food, too. Insects do not see the hidden geckos until it is too late to get away.

The Giant gecko's brown skin helps camouflage this species on tree branches.

Some desert geckos also rely on camouflage to trick their enemies. It is difficult to spot a Banded gecko in its desert habitat. Its yellow and brown skin blends well with the sand and rocks where it lives.

Predators make life difficult for both desert and tropical geckos. But life is easier for lizards in

Life in the Tropics

the tropics because of the warm climate and the rich supply of food. Nocturnal geckos need to live in places that stay warm even at night. And gecko eggs survive best in warm, moist places. Abundant food and mild weather in the tropics help explain why most geckos are found in these regions of the world.

This Giant Madagascan day gecko began its life inside a tiny, shelled egg.

Chapter 4

From Egg to Adult

Whether a gecko lives in a forest, a desert, a jungle, or a swamp, it has many things in common with other geckos. One of these is the way in which it began its life—inside a remarkable shelled egg.

Adult females of nearly all species of gecko lay eggs. Only a few species in New Zealand give birth to live young. The eggs remain inside the bodies of these female lizards until the babies hatch.

Male and female geckos often look alike. A male gecko must first find a female gecko of his species. If he spies another gecko in his territory, he makes noises and movements to get the other gecko to leave. A male will leave. But a female reacts differently. She moves close to the male and nudges him. This means she is ready to mate.

Two Hard-Shelled Eggs

Several days or weeks after mating—depending on the species—female geckos usually lay two small eggs. Females of smaller species, such as the Reef gecko, lay only one egg. The Reef gecko egg is as tiny as a pea! The average gecko egg is about 1 inch (2.5 centimeters) long and white or yellow-white in color.

Tropical geckos mate and lay eggs throughout the year. In cooler climates, geckos mate and lay eggs only in the spring. This way, the young geckos hatch during warmer months when there is more food to eat.

The female gecko looks for the right place to lay her eggs. She searches for a spot that is warm, moist, and safe from predators. She hides the eggs in the ground, or under rocks or bark. The females of some species lay their eggs together and share a nest.

A female Leopard gecko from Pakistan guards her two eggs.

The Gecko

After laying her eggs, the female leaves. Unless the eggs are eaten by predators, they will continue to live without any help from their mother.

Inside the Egg

Inside each gecko egg is a growing **embryo** and the nutrients that it needs until it is fully developed. The sturdy shell protects the contents from becoming too dry.

The new gecko begins as a group of living cells. Nutrients in the yolk, such as fats and proteins, help the cells to grow. As the embryo grows larger, the yolk gets smaller. The cells divide into different body organs—the heart, brain, bone, and muscle. Four little bulges on the embryo grow into legs. The embryo begins to look like a tiny gecko.

A gecko egg usually hatches in three months. Some species hatch in just four weeks, but a few others take almost seven months.

One day, a crack appears on the shell. The gecko pecks with its **egg tooth** to break out. The

From Egg to Adult

sharp egg tooth is attached to the baby's nose. It is larger than the other teeth inside its mouth. The egg tooth will fall out a few days after hatching. Its only purpose is to help the baby gecko work its way out of the shell and into the world.

Growing Up

The gecko **hatchling** takes its first breath of air as soon as it breaks out of its shell. Almost immediately, the baby moves quickly, chasing and eating small insects for its first meals.

From the start, the hatchling avoids harsh sunlight. But after a few months, the young gecko may join other geckos in feeding and sunbathing. Gradually, it chooses a feeding area that becomes its own territory. As an adult, the gecko will spend most of its time alone in this territory, except during the mating season.

Geckos grow rapidly. Newborns are about 1 to 2 inches (2.5 to 5 centimeters) long. By the age of six months, most have doubled in size. Within one

When the gecko is a few months old, it comes out of the shade for the first time to warm itself in the sun.

From Egg to Adult

to three years, they usually reach their full size. The lizards are now grown-up members of the gecko family. They are surviving on their own in the jungle, the desert, or the rain forest—just as their parents did.

Chapter 5

People and Geckos

Do geckos bring good luck or bad? People around the world have different answers to this question.

Although geckos do not harm humans, people in some parts of Asia fear them. They think that geckos are poisonous and carry diseases. These beliefs may be the result of old folktales. In one tale, a poisonous lizard could kill a person just by biting his shadow!

Other people like having geckos around. In the East Indies, people think that geckos bring good luck. In Malaysia and Java, new home owners believe that having a Tokay gecko in their house will bring them happiness.

People buy geckos as pets, hoping the lizards will kill unwanted insects in their homes. Certain

In the countries where the Indo-Pacific gecko lives, people believe it and other geckos bring good luck.

Most geckos do not like to be held, but this Texas Banded gecko does not seem to mind.

species, such as the Tokay gecko, Flying gecko, and house gecko, are sold in pet stores in the United States. The Tokay gecko is noisy and may bite when it is angry.

At times, these pets hide, and their owners have trouble catching them. Geckos do not like to be held. They may shed their tails or pieces of

People and Geckos

skin, trying to get away. Geckos are certainly not cuddly pets!

A Shrinking Habitat

Yeck-oh! Yeck-oh! To-kay! Churr-upp! The amazing, noisy gecko has survived for millions of years in a variety of places. But in some regions, people have become enemies of this loud, little lizard.

Humans have destroyed areas of the gecko's tropical forest habitats. Millions of acres of trees have been cut for lumber and other wood products, and to clear land for farms. Can the gecko continue to survive in spite of the changing conditions around it?

Today, four species of geckos are thought to be nearly **extinct**. The United States Fish and Wildlife Service includes the Monito gecko, Serpent Island gecko, and two kinds of day geckos in its list of **endangered** species.

The Monito gecko is a rare species. It lives on Monito, a small Caribbean island. Scientists believe

The Gecko

that Monito geckos and their eggs are being killed by a growing number of rats on the island. People are studying this problem. They hope to find out how many Monito geckos are still alive and to plan ways to save the species.

The three other endangered species live on an island country called Mauritius in the Indian Ocean. Geckos on Mauritius are prey to a growing number of rats. Rabbits and goats create another problem for them—they eat the green plants in the geckos' habitats.

The endangered day geckos on Mauritius are arboreal. They have suffered from the large number of palm trees cut down in this region during the past twenty years.

Once, northern Mauritius was almost covered with palms. Then, hundreds of acres of the trees were cut down to make room for houses, and tea and sugar fields. The lizards' habitat was shrinking, and many were dying. As a result, these species of geckos are almost extinct.

People and Geckos

The Future of the Gecko
In the years ahead, the survival of endangered geckos will depend upon human efforts to save their habitats. Today, many people around the world are trying to protect the forests of Africa and tropical America. **Conservation** organizations and the governments of certain countries, such as Costa Rica, are working together toward this goal.

Many scientists, too, are trying to save this small lizard. Some day geckos have been captured and taken to protected areas. As scientists, conservation organizations, and the governments of many countries work together, there is hope that the endangered species will survive.

The nimble gecko is a remarkable member of the animal kingdom. With help and protection from humans, its noisy call will continue to be heard in warm regions around the world, for many years to come.

Glossary

arboreal (ahr-BORE-eeh-uhl)—living in trees

camouflage (CAM-uh-flahj)—an appearance, especially color, that blends with the surroundings and may serve to conceal, or hide, an animal

cones—sense cells in the eye

conservation (kahn-sur-VAY-shuhn)—the preservation and protection of living things and their natural habitats

egg tooth—a sharp tooth on the snout of a lizard used to break out of its shell when hatching

embryo (EM-bree-oh)—a developing animal inside an egg during the early stages before birth

endangered—an animal or plant having a population so low that it is in danger of becoming extinct

extinct (ehk-STINGKT)—no longer living anywhere on earth; many plant and animal species have become extinct

hatchling—a creature that has recently hatched from an egg

herpetologist (hur-puh-TAHL-uh-jihst)—a scientist who studies reptiles

keratin (KARE-uht-uhn)—a tough, outer layer of cells found in fingernails, feathers, and horns

microscope—an instrument that makes objects look larger; used to look at tiny objects that cannot be seen with the eye alone

nocturnal (nock-TURN-uhl)—active during the night

nutrient (NOO-tree-ehnt)—a vitamin, mineral, protein or other substance found in food that helps support a living person, animal, or plant

order—a group of related people, animals, or things; lizards and snakes belong to the same order

parasite (PAIR-uh-site)—tiny creatures, such as mites, that live on larger animals; mites and other parasites feed on the larger animal, sucking its blood

predator (PREHD-uh-tuhr)—an animal that hunts other animals for food

prehensile (pree-HEN-suhl)—able to seize or grasp by wrapping around; a prehensile tail wraps around tree branches or leaves and helps the animal keep its balance

prey—an animal that is hunted by another animal for food

rain forest—a dense, humid tropical forest; occurs in areas that have high rainfall throughout the year

rods—sense cells inside the eye that pick up faint light very well

species (SPEE-sheez)—distinct kinds of individual plants or animals that have common characteristics and share a common name

spectacles—transparent eyelids that cannot open or close

territory—an area of land; wild animals defend their territory from other animals of the same kind

Index

behavior, 10-11, 15, 16, 41-42
body heat, 21-22
calls, 9-12, 19, 31, 51
camouflage, 36-37, 38
claws, 13, 14, 30
climbing, 10
coloring, 25, 26, 28, 30, 31
conservation, 53
defenses, 15
dinosaurs, 21
eating habits, 17, 24, 26, 34
eggs, 39, 41, 42, 44
egg tooth, 44-45
embryo, 44
endangered species, 51-52
extinction, 51
eyes, 16, 17, 28
feet, 12, 13, 28
folktales, 49
habitat, 13, 22, 28, 33, 34, 39, 51, 53
hatchlings, 33, 45, 47
herpetologists, 24
keratin, 23
mating, 11, 24
nests, 42
parasites, 24
pets, 49-50
predators, 10, 35-36, 38, 52
prey, 34
rain forest, 9
relatives, 21
scales, 23
shedding, 23, 24
size, 19, 25, 26, 28, 31
skin, 22-23
species, 11-12, 24, 25-28, 30-31
spectacles, 16-17
tail, 15, 19, 26-27, 28, 50
territory, 9-10, 19, 45
toe pads, 12, 14, 17

About the Author

A lifelong student of nature, Victoria Sherrow received her Bachelor of Science and Master of Science degrees from Ohio State University. Today, she is a member of several environmental groups, including the Audubon Society and the National Wildlife Federation. Ms. Sherrow is also a member of the Society of Children's Book Writers. She has written many articles and short stories for children's magazines. *The Gecko* is her third book for children. Ms. Sherrow lives in Westport, Connecticut, with her husband and three children.